WOLVES

POST CARD

First published 2005 by
MACMILLAN
Children's Books
a division of Macmillan Publishers Limited

This edition published 2006
by Macmillan Children's Books
20 New Wharf Road, London N1 9RR
Basingstoke and Oxford
Associated companies throughout the world
www.panmacmillan.com

ISBN-13: 978-1-4050-5362-4
ISBN-10: 1-4050-5362-3

THIS SPACE MAY BE USED FOR
PRINTED OR WRITTEN MATTER

For
Oleander Grrrabbit
(because I love you)
and the pottery pals
(because I promised)
X X X

A CIP catalogue record for this book is available from the British Library.

NEW IN AT YOUR LIBRARY!

WOLVES

Emily Grrrabbit

Burrow WOLVES and many other rip-roaring tails at your local library NOW!

MACMILLAN CHILDREN'S BOOKS

Rabbit went to the library.
He chose a book about . . .

WOLVES

GREY WOLVES live in packs of
between two and ten animals.

They can survive almost anywhere:
from the Arctic Circle . . .

. . . to the outskirts of towns and villages.

In some areas wolves have retreated
to places where fewer people live,
such as forests and woodland.

They have sharp claws . . .

. . . bushy tails . . .

. . . and dense fur, which harbours fleas and ticks.

An adult wolf has 42 teeth.
Its jaws are twice as powerful
as those of a large dog.

Wolves eat mainly
meat. They hunt
large prey such
as deer, bison and
moose.

They also enjoy
smaller mammals,
like beavers, voles
and . . .

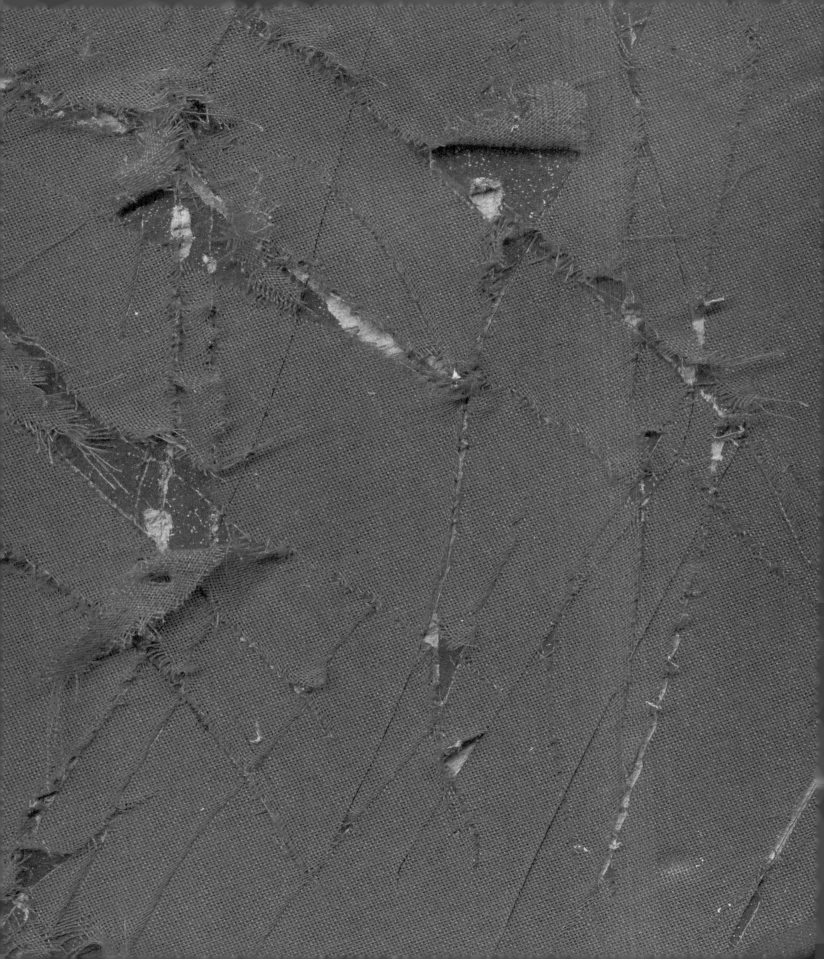

. . . rabbits.

The author would like to point out
that no rabbits were eaten during
the making of this book.
It is a work of fiction.
And so, for more sensitive readers,
here is an alternative ending.

Luckily this wolf was a vegetarian, so they shared a jam sandwich, became the best of friends, and lived happily ever after.

If undelivered please return to
West Bucks Public Burrowing Library
36 Warren Wood
Nibbleswick

Burrow more books

Burrowed Wok

Carrotenese Take Away

43 RABBIT RUN • THE HUTCH
DITCHLING ROAD • SALAD PATCHAM
TELEPHONE ORDERS WELCOME
TELEPHONE 260497

DELIVERY SERVICE AVAILABLE
7 EVENINGS A WEEK
From: 5.30pm – 11.00pm
Within 3 Miles £1.00, 4-5 Miles £1.50

FREE Lawn Crackers
on orders over £10

FREE Morning Dew
on orders over £30

• **OPENING HOURS** •
Monday – Thursday   5pm – 11.30pm
Friday – Saturday   5pm –12 Midnight
Sunday   5pm – 11.00pm

Angora Organics
GARDENING CATALOGUE
Every seed you need for the perfect patch.

G. RABBIT
LANE'S END BURROW
THE LONG FIELD
NIBBLESWICK

RABBIT MAIL
POSTAGE PAID
HQ 6733
GREAT BURROW

Open Air 2004
Mai – September
Museumsplatz Bonn

BRIEFZENTRUM 53

55€
DEUTSCHLAND

G RABBIT
LANE'S END BURROW
THE LONG FIELD
NIBBLESWICK
GREAT BURROW

Registered Office
The Den
High Hill

regards, Rabbit

PAY UP

This matter is now URGENT & is in your own
interest to contact us.
Please call us NOW on
0870 111011

merciless
final collections notice

JACK O'HARE
229 RABBIT RUN
THE BIG APPLE   01108
NIP CODE

Mr G Rabbit
Lane's End Burrow
The Long Field
NIBBLESWICK
GREAT BURROW

22 USA
22 USA

VIA HARE MAIL
CORREO AEREO
PAR AVION

BUCKSPOOL

NEW ZEALAND
PAID
99466
9.9.9
POSTAGE

long field
'swick

RÉPUBLIQUE FRANÇAISE
£3
NANTES
ROMAIN   17H   0003,00
26/09   602 PO4926
44100   LA POSTE

M. G. Rabbit
Lane's End Burrow
The Long Field
Nibbleswick

BY AIR MAIL
PAR AVION
MIT LUFTPOST